FOR MY PUP, LOUIE, AND HIS EPIC EARS

Library of Congress Cataloging-in-Publication Data
Anderson, Derek, 1969- author, illustrator.
Ten pigs / Derek Anderson. — First edition.   pages cm
Summary: One pig looks to take a relaxing bath in private, but he is soon
joined by another pig, then another, until there are ten pigs—and number
one has to come up with a plan so that he can actually enjoy his bath.
ISBN 978-0-545-16846-5
1. Counting—Juvenile fiction. 2. Swine—Juvenile fiction. 3. Stories in
rhyme. [1. Stories in rhyme. 2. Pigs—Fiction. 3. Baths—Fiction. 4. Counting.]
I. Title.   PZ8.3.A5453Te 2015   [E]—dc23   2014030750

10 9 8 7 6 5 4 3 2 1   15 16 17 18 19
Printed in Malaysia 108
First edition, May 2015

The text and display type was set in El Grande.
Book design by Charles Kreloff and David Saylor

The pictures for this book were created with ink, Photoshop, and soap suds.

TEN PIGS

AN EPIC BATH ADVENTURE

STORY AND PICTURES BY
DEREK ANDERSON

ORCHARD BOOKS • NEW YORK • AN IMPRINT OF SCHOLASTIC INC.

ONE PIG.

ONE **VERY** HAPPY PIG.

BUT ALONG COMES PIG NUMBER TWO.

THIS IS A BATH, NOT THE DEEP BLUE SEA!

THIS TUB IS TOO FULL.
THAT'S IT, NO MORE. OH NO!
HERE COMES PIG NUMBER
FOUR.

SEVEN
LAUNCHES HIS BOAT
WITH A SAILOR'S
SALUTE.

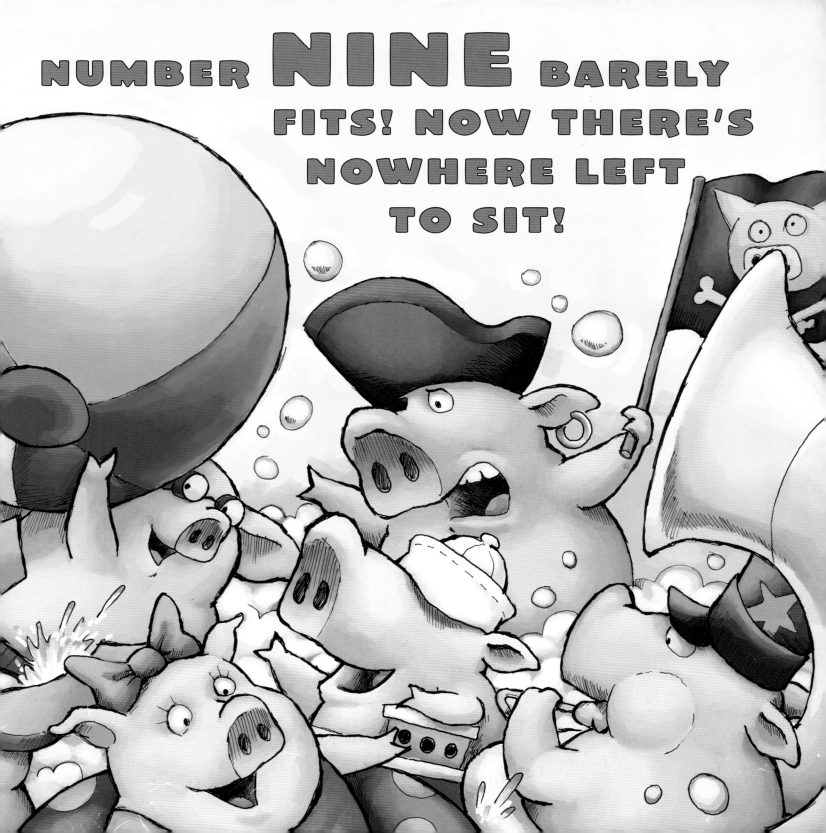

AND **TEN?**
NUMBER TEN WIGGLES
AND SQUEEZES AND
SURFS HIS WAY IN.

NO PIGS, NONE.

ONE WOLF.

ONE **VERY** HAPPY . . .

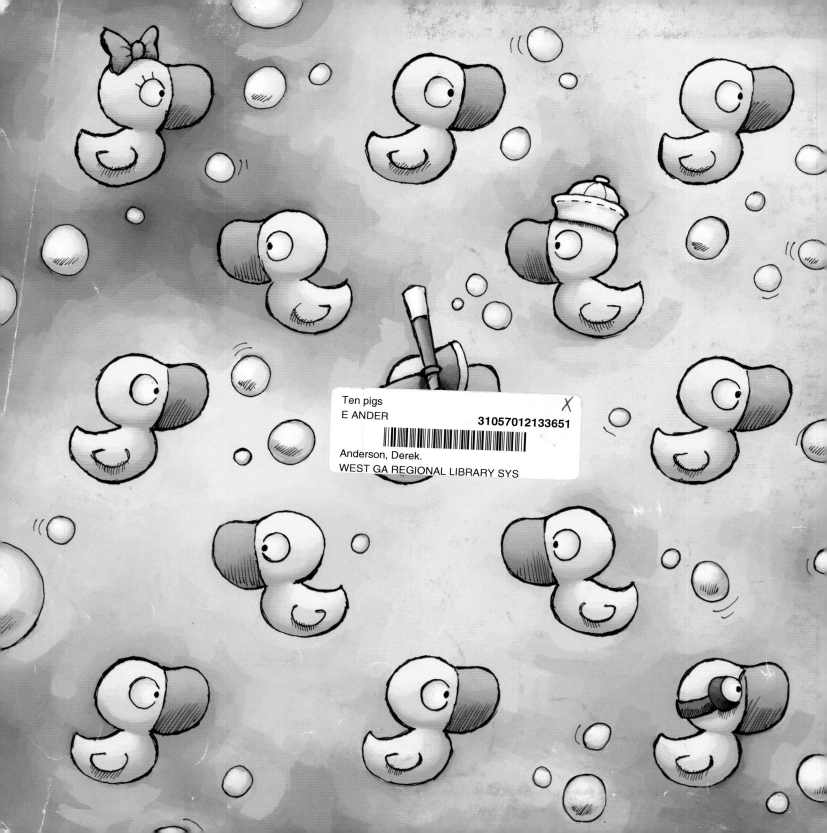